Trapped!

Is a collection of short stories by the talented writers of the 2018-19 Giraffes class of Marcham Primary School. All profits will be given to Painting for Freedom, a charity which supports Freeset. Freeset is a 'freedom business' that transforms the lives of women in India who have a very difficult life.

To find out more visit:

www.paintingforfreedom.co.uk

Trapped!

Edited by Lisa Lowe

First published in 2019 by Painting for Freedom
136 Old Road, Whaley Bridge, SK23 7LA
United Kingdom

www.paintingforfreedom.co.uk

ISBN 978-1-9160454-1-5

Contents

FREDDY'S

'STAY CALM IN THE SUITS'

by Alex Green

"*An abandoned restaurant named Freddy Fazbender's Pizza was located in the woods today. Scientists say trees have grown round it and the buildings surrounding it have rotted away. They don't know why it hasn't rotted too but some people think that-*"

"Stupid news," said Frits.

Frits was a thirteen year old boy with an orange fringe. He was normally miserable and or curious. He had three other friends: Susie, Jeremy and Fred. Jeremy had long black hair and he always wore blue sunglasses everywhere. Susie had blond hair and if she didn't have a ponytail it's not Susie. Fred was crazy. He has messy brown hair.

The next day Frits got to school and everyone was talking about Freddy's. The gang (Fred, Susie, Jeremy and Frits) other than Frits, who was more grumpy than ever, wanted to go explore the building. Frits wasn't sure at first but then he realized the popularity he'd get and all the cool stuff he'd collect so he agreed.

"Were going today.5:30 my house. Bring your bike and a flashlight. I don't think the lights will be on," mumbled Susie in her squeaky voice.

They all met up at the destination with their bikes. "The trek has begun!" said Frits. After an hour of riding it became dark and foggy but the gang had made it to the pizzeria.

"Is this it?" said Jeremy.

"I think so. The names there, the giant bear heads there, the mouldy black 'n' white walls are there so yep, it's the right place," replied Frits. They entered through the cracked glass door. The roof was leaking and gunk hung from the ceiling. Three animatronics stood on a stage – a chicken, a bear and a bunny. Off in the corner was a purple tent. Fred opened it and a pirate fox thing stood next to a carnival game.

"YARG. Win a prize any prize," the mangled animatronic said.

"AHH," Fred jumped back in fear as Susie noticed a door camouflaged in the wall. She entered with caution but the room was an office. It had a tape on the floor. She played it: "Hello and welcome to your job. Your job is to not let the animatronics move. They only move at 12AM 'till 6AM. If they get close to your doors, shut the doors. That's pretty much it. Not that hard right? Well, I'll let you decide. Goodbye.

They entered the 'parts and service' room. It just had plastic animal heads on shelves and a rusty metal skeleton.

"Let's go," said Frits.

"And where do you think you're going?" laughed a new-comer.

"Who are you?" said Jeremy.

"Leave us alone!" said Susie.

The voice walked towards the stage – where the gang have hid.

"There's a switch here," panted Fred.

      'Click' the robots back opened. Fred stepped in. Gears and wires were inside. Fred told everyone to enter as well. Frits, who was hiding behind the fox thing, found it out by himself. The doors shut. There was no escape. It was cramped for all of them. The gears were closing in.

CRUNCH.

"Stay calm in the suits..."

by Alistair France

The tree came down–THUD. Beep beep beep. Tim woke up, a dream still vaguely clinging on in his head. Tim, a quick skinny boy, was very independent due to the fact that his mother was ill and his father dead. He had blond wiry hair that grew in thick layers on top of his pale freckly face. Tim didn't go to school. He had to work so he could afford to pay for his food and his mother's medicine. Despite the fact of being poor, Tim had lots of friends due to his kindness and bravery. He looked around his tiny dirty room. He went to check on his Mum; she was still very ill. "Do you want me to get the shopping Mum?" asked Tim soothingly.

"That would be very kind of you dear," replied his Mum. Tim set out on his skateboard - like he did every morning–the cool breeze whipped his face waking him very efficiently. He whizzed past the brightly coloured stalls gleaming in the bright sunlight. The smell of spices filled the air with mouth-watering smells. He passed all these nice stalls till he came across a purple tent with a magnificent coat of arms on the opening of the tent. Tim walked into the magnificent tent; there were lots of mini, colourful tents with the same coat of arms on the front of them. This was the purple market. There was a section for everything: there were medicine stalls, food and more. Tim went into the medicine stall for his mum and went into the food stall for the groceries. Shopping finished, Tim started to walk back to the entrance when out of the corner of his eye he spotted a small orange tent that hadn't been there when he had walked past the first time. It looked like a giant face with windows for eyes and a sideways door for a mouth.

All of a sudden he had a sudden sensation to go inside. He wasn't sure about going in: the shop looked like a face. He cautiously edged his way closer towards the sideways door. As soon as he was about to touch the handle, the door turned up-right. Tim was more nervous than he'd ever been in his entire life; the door had just opened and kept swinging to beckon him inside. He stepped inside. The first door shut behind him and turned sideways. He stealthily nudged open the second door. It opened. He could hear the hail pounding on the roof of the satsuma like tent. He stepped through. A room of wonder came into vision.

There were two wooden train tracks; one with a blue train the other with a green. There was a china doll sat with teddy bears having a picnic. It even felt like they were watching him. The walls were bright pink and there was a tower of ginger building blocks in one corner.

After a bit of snooping around, he spotted a doll's house full of real moving dolls. He decided to take a closer look at this interesting artefact. Inspecting it, he noticed that the dolls were dancing on a ballroom floor and that the two royal looking figures gave a speech which when they finished the room erupted with a loud cheer. Huge tables were brought into the hall by lots of servants with long tights and collars. He realised it was the Tudors and they were doing the same things over and over again.

Shaking off what he had just seen he went to turn back, but the door was locked. He slumped against the door. Pounding, he tried to break free. Looking for a way out, Tim spotted a wooden pillar with engravings on it. He went to go and look at it when he tripped over the doll's house and he got sucked into the pillar. A blue mist swept around him and clocks ticked backwards. Suddenly he fell into a bramble bush watching a man cut down a birch tree. Bang! It hit the forest floor. He was in the same room, door still locked. He blinked.

The tree came down THUD! Beep beep beep. Tim woke up. He wasn't in his bedroom; or even his house. He was in a strange room with pink walls and two train tracks one with a blue train and one with a green one. Somehow he had moved away from his house with his bed and his alarm clock and was in a strange room with no windows and no doors. In one corner there stood a tall pillar with engravings on. He walked closer and gets sucked into the pillar. A blue mist swept around him. There were names and his name was right in the middle of the pillar. He tripped over a doll's house and clocks ticked back. He was in a bramble bush watching a man get ready to cut down a birch tree. Tim had a funny feeling he had seen this before; before he woke up.

As if by instinct, he leapt out of the bush and took the man's equipment and ran. Sweat trickled down his forehead and adrenalin was causing him to stumble. The man was close behind him. He ran twisting and turning though the maze of trees until he came across a door. He opened it and jumped through. He was back in the room; except that his bed was gone and his clock and the pillar not forgetting the doll's house he tripped over. Suddenly the walls around him began to fade.

He was delighted to be back outside. In place of the giant satsuma shop stood a giant tree; in fact it was a giant birch tree. The smell of the air was delightful. Then he realised: it was dusk. He had spent a whole day shopping. His mum would be worried sick. He ran home as fast as he could go. When he got home, he apologised for being late but his mum said, "You've only been gone two hours."

"What had happened?" wondered Tim.

by Amy McNeil

"Caddy, I'm bored."

"You won't be when we've found this book. Come on!"

Caddy and Emilie Tintal lived in Fumberland House. It was a big estate with a huge library – it was seldom that they ever found anything they wanted. Although, it did have some great books. Caddy was trying to find 'Alice in Wonderland' for Emilie. It was a classic and she thought Emilie might like it. It was taking ages though, it was no surprise: the library was massive. Their parents weren't there to help them. They never were. They were always away exploring; even when they came home their feet were itching to go away again. It wasn't that they didn't love them – they knew they loved them. Maybe they just didn't like the house; hopefully.

"What's that?"

"What's what?"

"Over there! A glowing book!"

"Stop being silly Em...wait...what is that?"

"It's a glowing book, silly. Come on. Let's read that one."

"Wait. I don't think it's a good idea." But she had already strode off. Bother. That was so like Emilie. Then, as she was pulling it, an outline of a door shimmered into a solid, wooden door.

"Oooh. Let's open it."

"No! Emilie don't do it!" But she'd already gone and opened the door.

Now Caddy had a choice: would she go through with Emilie or would she not. Going through with Emilie seemed the better choice but was it? She didn't know. Eventually, she decided to go to Emilie, after all, what could happen?

Stepping through the threshold, she strode forward into the room. Emile was nowhere to be seen. There were clocks everywhere. They lined the walls; were on the shelves and the great grand-father clocks stood tall as they leaned against the clock-covered walls. The wallpaper, that you could barely see, was peeling and was a discoloured yellow. The faded toads peered at her through beady, paper eyes. Then, in the corner, an old man that had wispy hair sat with a ponderous expression on his face. He was sat on one of the lime-green, velvet armchairs; his legs crossed; his arms folded.

"You are too late. She has already fallen into the trap," he rasped.

"What trap? I don't know of any trap," she whispered back.

"The trap you are about to fall into too." After saying the last word he vanished into thin air.

"Is it just me, or is everything turning zany?" she asked herself.

Then, she saw the pocket watch. It was a reasonable size with large engravings. The numbers were Roman Numerals. Forgetting what the old man told her, Caddy's insides tingled with temptation; she just had to touch that watch and everything would be fine. She was sure of it.

Suddenly, the lights started to dim. Caddy shivered.

Was this the right thing to do after all? She wasn't sure. Still, she kept on walking – quieter though, more careful. Just a bit further. There. She touched it.

Terror took hold of her; it was like her insides were being sucked out. Then, everything stopped. Caddy looked down on herself. She was transparent! After that, she observed her surroundings, and there was Emilie – looking like a ghost – sitting in the corner.

The wall was old cogs stuck together and the floor was similar. It was cramped in there; about the size of a large cupboard. Then she realised. She was in the pocket watch. She was sad that she wouldn't see any more of her parents but at least she had Emilie.

Yes, at least she had Emilie.

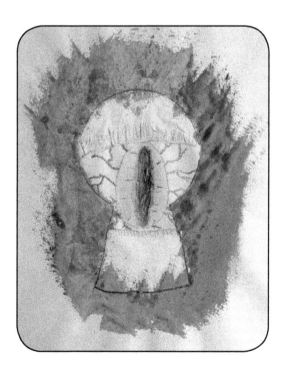

Room No3

by Angela Cao

Hot tears fall down my face. She's ill now and it's all my fault. The ambulance's sirens scream in my ears and I can't bear to see her go. I feel a hand wrap around my shoulder.

"It's all right." No it's not. Dad doesn't understand. It's not that simple. They load her into the ambulance and drive off. I run off back into the house.

The next day, I'm driven off to my grandparents. Dad's too busy to look after me. I don't need him anyway. I try to convince myself that I'm better off without him. It doesn't work. I catch the driver looking at me through the

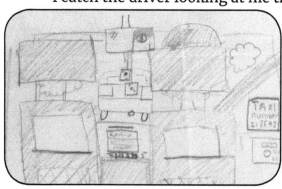

mirror. Probably wondering why I am here. What I am doing. But he doesn't ask. I pull a face at him and he looks away quickly. For the rest of the journey, I just stare at the two dice that are both on three. We finally arrive. His house is so much larger than I remembered. The driver gets out and whispers something to Grandpa. He nods and the driver gets back in the car and hints for me to get out. Suddenly I'm shaking. This was Grandpa, the husband of my lovely Grandma. Yet he was so unfamiliar. I clamber out, reaching for my case on my seat.

He smiles at me briefly, muttering to himself under his breath. There is an awkward few moments when I try to think of something to say.

"So u...m...m..., how's Grandma?" His face darkens when I ask and I know I've asked the wrong question. So the rest of the time is spent in silence. I rub my hand against the hard leather of my suitcase.

She arrived around early morning. She comes in a dirty yellow taxi and I see her gawping at the house. The driver comes out and asks me if I'm expecting her. I nod and watch as she gets out. I grin at her quickly. Then it hit me: she looked so much like her gran. I look down to stop my eyes from watering. Slowly, I opened the door. She looks at me then she speaks.

"How's Grandma?" It's blurted out and almost innocently. Memories flood back to me. Her smile, her emerald eyes, silky red hair. How her eyes twinkled. How she talked. I walk up the stairs and show her to her room then I make myself a cup of tea and sit at the table. I can't believe what just happened.

He just dropped me off into my room. All he said was:

"You're free to explore, just don't go into the third level." Then I heard him trundle downstairs and switch on the kettle. I settle down onto the hard wooden bed and close the curtains. I nestle deep within the covers and lull myself to sleep even though it's still morning. It stops me from thinking about mum. I persuade myself to believe everything is fine but it isn't.

I wake up and its morning. I slept in my clothes. I rolled out of bed; attempting to stand up. I smoothed down my fiery hair and glance round for a mirror. Nope. I pulled off my crumpled clothes and grabbed some from my open suitcase. I don't remember leaving it open. I rummage around to see if anything was missing. My compact mirror. I'm sure it will turn up. I tidy my room and pull open the curtains. I blink at the beaming sun. And the trees wave at me. 3 birds fly by. I pull open the door and step into the hallway. Instead of going downstairs to breakfast, I find myself walking up the stairs to the next level. The walls are decked with framed pictures; all the pictures are coated in a layer of dust. I brush away the dust and stare at the picture. It's a person with a royal blue and gold mask and golden hair. But then I don't stop. My legs drag me up the stairs and onto the 3rd floor. Grandpa's voice echoes through my head.

"Don't go on the 3rd floor." But I ignore it. It wouldn't be that bad. Would it? Maybe it would. I resist the urge to discover and go back downstairs. I glance at the calendar as I go by. Today's date is circled and rewritten. The 3rd of March. However I am too starving to linger any longer. I go into the kitchen and pour myself a cup of juice as I watch grandpa fry bacon and eggs. Something about today felt weird. The old grandfather clock in the living room chimed nine chimes.

I'm frying bacon and eggs when she comes in. She helps herself to juice and slumps down on a chair. The clock chimes nine times. I hear Sophie's cup slam down.

I finish my breakfast and go back to my room to avoid talking to Grandpa. Guilt floods into me when I hear him call me but I don't stop. I can't face him. The weird nagging feeling takes over and I walk up to the 3rd floor. My face burns. I don't know what I'm doing but for some reason I feel like need to go to the 3rd floor. No turning back now. When I reach the 3rd floor, I suddenly feel a wave of calmness wash over me. The carpet is soft and plush and I wriggle my toes in it. The wallpaper is painted blue with white diamonds. I slow down as I reach the first door. A sneering ugly mask is stuck to the door with a '1' on its forehead. I tug at the door but it wouldn't budge. So I move onto the next. This time it has a sad mask. Half blue and half green.

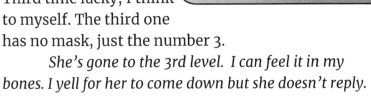

A tear is frozen on the upper cheek. The eyes are full of sadness. No. 1 says the sign. I pull the knob but it's stuck. Third time lucky, I think to myself. The third one has no mask, just the number 3.

She's gone to the 3rd level. I can feel it in my bones. I yell for her to come down but she doesn't reply. I walk to the stairs and wait for a noise. Nothing. Then click.

I tug at the 3rd door, already knowing the result. The brass handle doesn't budge. Tears grow in my eyes. Then I remember something the teacher made me read when I was younger. About picking locks. I pulled a hair pin out. I held my breath as I inserted my pin. Nothing. I should have known better. Obviously it doesn't work. I was so stupid for believing it. I curse myself under my breath. I turned back, away from the room. Then the door clicked. It creaked as if it had been closed for a thousand years. My anger immediately melted into curiosity as I tip-toed in. Light blinded me. And I didn't dare to breathe. When my eyes adjusted, I gasped at the sight that lay before me. It was a ginormous ballroom. Around the room were four floor to ceiling windows and two glittering chandeliers. The ceiling was covered with gold swirly patterns. I always used to play in this house with Grandma but I never heard of this one before. For a second I imagine what it would be like to dance in here. Why would Grandpa hide this magnificent room from me? I picture mum dancing with me and smiling her sunshine smile. I look into the big ornate mirror. My red hair curls too much and my eyes are too round. In the back of the room, I catch a glimpse of something.

There was a clothes rail in the corner. It was overfilled with dresses and suits. One of them caught my eye. A flowy dress hung in the middle. It was light blue with gold sequins piled so it filled the top then separated near the bottom. My hands twitched. Surely Grandpa wouldn't mind just one try. I mean I did find this room. I grabbed it and got changed into it. I loved the feeling of it as it flowed. I peeked in the ornate mirror. My red hair bounced around my shoulders and my green eyes glittered. If only mum could see me now. She would be proud. A pang of guilt hit me as I remembered mum was ill. Suddenly everything went dark. I reached round and felt for a switch. I flicked it. All I could see was masks. They were laughing. At me. I closed my eyes and hugged my knees. I wasn't sure what happened but knew I was stuck. Trapped.

Burning Canvas
by Aoife Marah

"Hey, little Tommy. Here, have some food!" One crisp, autumn morning, my ginger tom bathed in the golden light of the rising sun. The lazy cat rolled over and purred as he was tickled. I had ebony hair, tied into neat braids, and wore a simple T-shirt, cardigan and worn out jeans. My dark, smooth skin was pierced viciously down my left cheek with a ferocious scar. The cramped attic room was far from luxurious but, at dawn, it was a lovely place to be. It was moments like these when my dark, smoky past was forgotten. Then, when the sun was high, I realised. I cried.

My parents had been missing for six months. Six months since... then. They were probably dead. All I had was my cat, my only friend. Tommy was a gift from my Mother on my 9th birthday and had been with me for two years. He leapt onto the floor and padded down the narrow staircase. I could hear Susan downstairs, cooking. Susan had been very good to me and had cared for me since my parents went missing. She kept saying that the house wasn't big enough for both of us and I would have to leave eventually. I denied it but we both knew she was right. Below, there was a knock at the door and a kerfuffle as Tommy hooked his claws on it stubbornly. Eventually, the hinges creaked open and I heard a medley of voices.

"Hello...yes, of course... already?"

Then a new voice filled the house.

"Early? ...sorry! ...where is she? ... Sierra, yes."

Me. I am Sierra. I rushed down the stairs and into the hallway where a short lady stood proudly. Large, gold, hoop earrings hung from her ears. Her golden hair was neatly tied on the top of her head. Her wrinkled face was smothered in makeup and a short, flowery dress covered her body and added to her flamboyant appearance. Her clothes were brighter than anything I had seen before. Our eyes locked and a stony silence fell onto the room. Her eyelids twitched and a sour grimace struck her face but within a second, it was gone.

Susan told me that the lady`s name was Rosa Harwood and she was my new guardian. Although she looked far from friendly to me, Susan saw nothing but perfection in her. My suitcase was packed and I was sent to the hallway. A million questions fought for a place in my mind. What can I do? As I sat in the rusty, clunking car, I watched raindrops form patterns and race across the window. I focused on the sound of the stuttering engine as we trundled along. I felt the steady rock of the car as it lulled me to sleep. We screeched to a halt outside an enormous manor. Wooden carvings swirled and climbed along the gutter and ascended to the roof. Ivy covered the walls, smothering any trace of the red bricks below. It was unlike anything I had seen before. I pushed open the car door and stepped out, mesmerised. My feet crunched against the gravel path as I headed to the front door. I

pushed it open and stepped inside...

It was dark and dingy inside. Candles lit the hallway, dipping melted wax on the threadbare rug. I was shown to a musty, damp room. A small bed in the centre of the room creaked in the draft that blew through an open window. I shoved it closed and flopped on my bed. I slept.

In the morning, I woke up unusually cold. I sat up and looked at the end of my bed. It was empty. Tommy always slept at the end of my bed. Where was he? I remembered him slipping out the door in the evening, searching for mice. He must have got stuck outside when I shut the door. I clambered out of bed, pulled on my slippers and went to look for him.

Navigating through the gloomy corridors was difficult but I was determined to find him. As the hours passed, I grew concerned. I kept imagining his stone-cold, lifeless body, all alone.
No. He`s probably just chasing mice.

I opened an endless amount of doors, discovering rooms that had been deserted for years. Every door was unlocked except one. I wiggled and pulled the handle so hard that it almost fell off. Eventually, I gave up hope and traipsed the remaining corridors for any sign of a cat. I searched every dust-coated room, every rotting hall and

found myself back where I began. I called out for Rosa but I got no reply. I hadn`t seen her since we got to the house. I decided to investigate the locked room further.
I peeped through the keyhole. I focused my eyes to look past a cobweb and could make out the room behind. It was an art studio.

A rickety easel stood in front of piled-up pictures. Wooden floorboards lined the floor and I longed to enter. I used to do art every day, back then.I spent hours upon end creating my masterpieces, but then it was all gone. I felt a tear roll down my cheek and fall into my lap. I snapped back into reality. I turned my back on the door to look for a key. I thought it might be tucked under the door but nothing was there except a pile of dust. I slumped against the door, set to give up. The door swung open.

I stepped inside. A floor board creaked and a shiver went down my spine. I breathed in a thick, smoky scent. It reminded me of my past, the fire. It was the smell of burning canvas. Piles of rubbish covered the room, leaving only a small space for me to stand. Cobwebs filled the dark corners and recesses of the room. I ran my finger over grime-coated portraits as I walked, my eyes fixated on the very end of the room. There, in front of a pile of rubbish, was a sketchbook. It was bound in leather and its cover seemed to glow in the darkness. I couldn't help myself. I reached out and picked it up. It felt warm in my hand, as if it was meant to sit there. I felt the spine and carefully opened it...

I flicked through the pages. They were all pictures of people, screaming. Then I reached the middle of the book and there, drawn in black ink, was my dad. The next page was my mum. Then it was Rosa and finally, Tommy. I turned the page again. It was blank. Suddenly, a piercing headache hit me like a wave. I shook violently and collapsed on the floor. As my eyes closed, I saw that a drawing now filled the empty page: a drawing of me.

Now I am trapped.

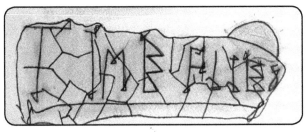

by Bethan Platt

Callum was an odd boy. A boy like no other. He stood out of the crowd like a pink pea in a green pod. How do I know this? I have been watching him his whole entire life. From the second he was born to now. My name you might ask is Nobody. Callum has no idea that I exist. But –unfortunately- he has no idea what will happen in the next two weeks...

Callum struggled with packing tops, trousers and socks into his old battered suitcase. Callum has been through a lot in his life. His mother had sadly passed away when he was four – due to a car crash. Every day at school, he had to endeavour to hide the pain –that was growing and growing inside. All he could think about while he was packing was his Mother. You might also ask the question: why is he packing? I will tell you. Callum's Mother –as you know- has passed away, sadly, and his dad is very negligent; he doesn't look after Callum whatsoever. Everything he does, he does it alone. Every single meal he has eaten, he had made himself. Callum shoved the last pair of socks into his bag. Time to leave...

Callum struggled with his bag, down the stairs, with a THUD at every step. He craned his neck around the doorway and gazed at his dad –

who was staring into the screen of the television. His dad was always sat on the sequined sofa. Sometimes, he wishes he had a normal dad – like everyone else. But Callum wasn't normal. Nothing about him was normal. Nothing at all. Callum slowly sunk down onto the cold hard floor. He removed his old, battered trainers from the pile. Callum slowly tied his laces and pulled them so tight that he felt a shiver go up his leg. Once he had finished, he slowly walked into the living room dragging his feet behind him. "Bye!" Callum called out. No reply. "I guess I'll see you soon!" he called out again. Still no reply...

Callum walked up to the old door – that was covered in peeling paint. He opened it with tonnes of force and a gust of wind hit him in the face. His eyes started watering. Is this the cold or am I crying he thought? They were hot against his pale face. I'm crying he realised. The black gleaming taxi had arrived. He walked outside and carefully opened the taxi door revealing a, slightly less clean, interior.

Callum stepped inside preparing for the journey ahead. "You ready sir," asked the driver. "Yes," said Callum, not really sure that was the truth. The driver started the engine. They were off... It felt like a life time. Callum just daydreamed and stared out of the clear, shimmering window. Trees, birds and leaves shot past his eyes. Occasional flashes of grey, blue and black, which he assumed were cars, came whizzing past. The day was grey, dark and rainy. Callum heard huge raindrops thundering down on the roof of the car. It was getting louder and louder and now sounded like hail. Now it was even louder like thunder. Callum looked out the window. It was thunder. Streaks of lightning came crashing down and hit the grass.

Callum counted in his head: one...two... three...four. An explosion of lightning thundered in his ears. The storm wasn't that far away...

"We're here sir," said the taxi driver. "Thank you," replied Callum as polite as he could. "It's ok. 'njoy your journey," the driver shouted, so Callum could hear him. Callum forced the door shut and with a loud THUD it closed. Callum ran up to the engraved double doors, covering his head with his hands. The station had shiny floors and surfaces all gleaming in the light of the huge chandelier that was hanging on the wood swirled ceiling. "Wow," Callum thought. Suddenly, he heard a crackling sound and just after that, "Train twenty two leaving from platform ten in two minutes," a voice said. That was his train. Callum started running pell-mell down the shining corridor. People gave him strange looks as he ran past them. He focused his eyes onto the station. Run, run, run, Callum heard in his head. Out of breath, Callum skidded to a halt at the station. Relief flooded his head. Callum ran onto the train. The whistle screamed and the train jolted out of the station just in time.

Callum watched the nature out of the murky, cracked window. Callum started to wonder about his mother. She was beautiful with long flowing black hair and eyes like diamonds. Hot tears trickled down his cold pale face. Callum felt himself drifting off deeper and deeper into sleep.

Callum was awoken by a screaming whistle and breaks so hard that they threw him forwards. He finally realised that they had arrived. Callum ran out of the train, his eyes still drooping. He didn't take the time to look at the view, but from the glimpse he saw he knew it was beautiful. Callum jogged down the street. He looked around for thirteen Bevilan Street. There it was. The numbers one three gleamed in the sunlight. Ivy crawled up the doors and windows. The door knocker was rusted and old. Callum walked up to the polished golden gates. This was it...

Callum swung the door knocker and it rattled against the peeling door. The double doors creaked open. "Hello!" shouted a man with a black beard looking very jolly.

"H-hi," Callum stuttered as he had no idea who this man was.

"Come in!" the jolly man bellowed, "Come in," the man said a little quieter to Callum's delight. "My name is Quinn," Quinn explained, "and this is my wife Violet." A little old dwarf lady with an arched back and a walking stick emerged from the darkness of the house. "And yours is?" Quinn asked.

"I'm Callum," he replied a little more confident this time. There was a weird silence that lasted around thirty seconds. "Anyway, anyway. Come inside!" Quinn said a little awkwardly "It's cold outside!" Callum looked behind him. The sun was out. Callum turned around slowly and looked a bit puzzled. Callum set foot in the house and his eyes widened. The house was ringing with beauty. This place was now his home. There was only one weird thing about this house. There were no clocks whatsoever...

"Your room is upstairs and to the right," Quinn explained, "But just before you go up there, there is one rule: don't go in the basement!" Quinn and Violet said in unison. A shiver crawled down his spine. As he went upstairs, he gulped. Once he was out of sight, he ran pell-mell up to his bedroom. Callum had no energy. He just collapsed onto his bed and felt himself drifting off deeper and deeper into sleep...

Callum was startled awake. Scratching, screaming and clawing. Where was it coming from? He listened harder. It was coming from the basement. Callum scrambled out of bed as quiet as he could. He stared out into the ebony sky and felt a strange feeling; he was being watched. Callum shook himself out of a daydream. He walked down the wooden spiral steps with a creak at every step. He was petrified.

When he finally got down, he headed straight to the trapdoor that lead to the basement. Callum ducked down and he scrambled through. It was pitch black. He fumbled around and found a light switch. Callum pulled it with all his might and the surprise threw him back. There were clocks. Thousands of clocks with eyes were all staring at him. But there was one clock that caught his attention. It was covered with a white cloth. He pulled it down. It was a grandfather clock engraved with beautiful patterns. It was magnificent. The light flickered like a burning candle. Hail thundered down on the window pain. Lightning stabbed across the blacked out sky. Callum reached out. He stretched out so much that all the muscles in his arm burned like a fire. He felt the cold wood press against his hand...

It was black. Pitch black. Callum could see nothing. Nothing at all. He tried to scream but there was nothing. Nothing at all. Callum could only hear one thing. All it was, was tick, tick, tick. Callum heard a cackling coming from outside. "I knew you would be nosy enough to come down," said the evil snarling voice, "Now this clock is your home..."

Soul

by Charlotte Wilson

English camp 1066

"What did you do? You have been away for hours," my father cried. Thud! An arrow hit the tree next to us. Twang! Another arrow hit a rope. We were under siege.

"You two get inside now," cried father.

"I want to stay," I protest. A rain of fiery arrows came down from the woods. They landed five hundred meters away. "On second thoughts I'll be inside." Fire raged and it was getting closer to our hiding place. My mother rushes in and shows us to a different place- a place in a hill. Mother rushes back to help father while leaving Beartrice and I shivering in the dark. My heart fills with ice. Even from here we can hear it- loud and clear. A scream. It shatters the night sky.

Beartrice is gone and I'm scared. I think she's scouting the area but I'm not sure. I go outside to check that she is there .She is not. "Where were you? You have been away for hours, we were getting worried," I sigh.

"I was only catching some food for us," she said sprinting up the hill. We are cooking rabbit and deer and chatting about stuff and then it comes round to my family. Beartrice acts as if it were a fairy tale: as if it weren't real. Beartrice doesn't care. She says she is

working on something with a friend. Her parents died in a fire like mine. We adopted her.

"We should move," she said, pointing to the trees.

"But that's the dark forest," I say, fear in my voice.

"Exactly," she said, "No-one goes there. It's time to pack up."

She has been acting strangely. Firstly, I'm her only friend, no other kids live around here. Secondly, she used to be scared and now she is brave. Last of all, she used to follow the rules and now she is a rebel. She is bustling around the cave whilst I'm scouting the area. I see our tent, a pile of ashes, glowing in the sunset. The Normans are searching the wreckage and I now know they would come for us next. That's why Beartrice wants to pack up so early. She wanted to get me away from them.

They zoomed into the woods. An arrow hit the tree next to them. Calisto and Beartrice looked around the trees. No-one was there. They needed to find somewhere to camp for the night. The ground was  littered with twigs. The trees were so close together that they couldn't see the sun. They rode on until the sun went behind the hill. They found a clearing that they could sleep in and agreed they could camp there.

Calisto then had the strangest dream...
There was a withered tent with the weirdest flag. The flag was red with a double bass on it with a sandy coloured whirlwind coming out of it. The tents walls were red and the sky was a funny shade of magenta.

The sky was the same colour as the tent. A tall man was standing by the tent door. He had sandy coloured hair. Just like Beartrice has. He disappeared into the trees.

"My Lord," said a girl's voice, "She is coming. I will bring her to you."

"No," said a raspy voice, "Let her come to me. Go. It is nearly dawn."

Then the tent magically moved forwards.

Calisto sat up and banged her head on the saddle of Ganymede. Calisto got up and searched for Beartrice. She was not there. An idea popped into her head. A frightful, nightmarish idea. Had Beartrice been caught by the man in her dream? Calisto saddled Ganymede, tied Iona to a tree and set off— being careful not to get ambushed by the Normans. The day turned to night but the animals stayed awake as if they were waiting to watch a spectacle. She came to a gap in the trees. The ground was strangely clean. A couple of seconds later, she knew why. A tent, just like the one in her dream had appeared. It was red with a strange pattern. The tent was made out of silk – light silk. The flag was stood straight as if it were being held up by an invisible person. The sky turned to magenta, the same colour as the tent.

The tent door opened and Calisto entered. A noise rang out: the sound of a tent door zipping up.

"Invite our guest in," said a raspy voice.

"Yes Lord," said the girl's voice, which sounded like Beartrice.

"Okay, it's just that you sound like my best friend Beartrice," mumbled Calisto.

Beartrice stepped forwards and said, "Come along to the music room. We have something to show you."

Calisto stepped into the room stumbling on some steps.

The room was stone and the stone was as cold as ice. This part was invisible to the outside world. She saw a musical instrument just like the one inside the tent when they were under siege. Calisto saw a double bass with engravings of her in the wood. She moved closer and heard whispers telling her not to come closer. The whispers sounded familiar like someone she knew all too well. Ignoring the whispers, she stepped closer. Her hand snaked towards the instrument. She touched it. Calisto felt like she was falling into nothingness. She let out a strangled scream.

Aaaaaaaaaaah!

Theme Park

by Cooper Harrison

One day I was jogging home from school. It was freezing. I could see an abandoned theme park. I went to investigate and I saw a ghost train. The ghost train had a giant land

mark on top and the carriages resembled a demon. It scared me but I still got on and started to look around. Just under one meter.

I was confused and petrified. Why was it crying? Is it a fake? No it must be real. I can see a tea-cup and piles of bones. I took a deep breath and shrugged it off. How is an old tea cup ride going to hurt me? Is that a watch? Yes that is a watch. Is that an antique watch by a rusty helter-skelter? There is a mannequin in the doorway. I might as well get it anyway. It might not be useless at all. I can tell all my friends at school and I'm going to brag about it.

They will really want it but no I'm not giving it to them. It is 11 o'clock. It strikes 12 o'clock. Tic toc tic toc.

Where am I? I can see clock hands. I think I'm trapped in my watch. My mum gives me my breakfast and all she saw was a watch. She was confused why I wasn't there...

Trapped

by Ellie Warwick

1968, Hawthorn orphanage

Thorn house- as people called it- was supposedly a homely place. There were warm fires, colourful walls and everything that should make somewhere comfy. But as you will later discover, lurking inside the walls, it wasn't. The once-painted gates were now a musty brown, precariously dangling off the hinges. Numerous chimney spouts spluttered out polluting gas that clogged the boy's lungs during lonesome afternoon walks. Even the presumably cheering pictures clinging to the peeling paint haunted the dreams of younger students. Everything had to fall under the limited mercy of the rules.

A thirteen year old boy, Tom, was sitting on one of the many windowsills of the orphanage. His mousy, brown curls covered his eyes as he pondered about life. This is where our story begins.

Breakfast was simple: pancakes - hairy, uncooked lumps served with lemon juice and sugar but without the sugar. Of course, you would scoff them up claiming (slightly too loudly) how delicious it was. All of this would take place at five a.m.

As for the rules, well you could replace all stupid one hundred with have a miserable life. Every boy had dared his peers to go onto the forbidden floor thirteen via the secret entrance. People claim that they have but it was a well-known fact that no-one ever dared.

As the boys trudged off to bed, Tom heard some muffled whispers coming from Sirs office. He couldn't help but overhearing.

"Yes, yes indeed. And that tragic scene of Christmas 1956."

Tom calculated he would have been less than one at the time.

"Thomas's parents I believe. Was it not?"

It must have been the booming voice of head boy, Fredrick. He was in room six. Tom however was in dorm thirteen. Everyone believed that thirteen was haunted. Tom knew it wasn't but had never not checked under his bed each night. But all of this was too much. Tom knew that his parents had died. But not at Christmas. Not near his first birthday. This news was lightening to his ears.

"Indeed. We still have the photo. That is, if you would like to see it. It is on floor thirteen." Sir was on the verge of awkward; something Thomas had never heard before.

Tom didn't catch the rest as the prefect of his room had come searching for him. Tom quickly ducked behind a vase. It was the most obvious space in the world. The prefect would see him immediately. The lights suddenly dimmed but surely that was just Tom's imagination. Yet the prefect walked straight past. Strange.

What had Sir said? We still have the painting? Or it might have been a picture, a page, or a note? Or

a photo? Yes that was it, a photo on floor thirteen.
Why did everything turn back to floor thirteen?

With quick realisation, Tom's surroundings
were alive. The ceiling was sloping downwards;
the whitewashed walls scratched against Tom's
itchy pullover. If a boy had strength - but more
the nerve- he could push a slab of the wall (that
is a trapdoor in reality) to the side. It was the only
unsealed entrance to

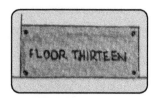

Tom was drawn; Tom crouched; he pushed it
to the side; he clambered in.

The walls, floors and shelves were smothered
in books, photos and papers. This must have
once been the store floor. He picked up a paper at
random. It was Arthur's birth certificate. The next
was one of the boys dressed in his Sunday best. It
might have been Bartholomew. How Tom could
mock the boys when he got back. He browsed the
shelves a little longer. A photo caught his eye.

It was a picture of a baby boy sitting on a
woman's knee. With a hand on her shoulders was a
proud man standing tall. It must be one of the boy's
family. Or at least used to be. He plucked it off the
wall and turned it over in his hands. Tom's heart
stopped beating. There was a message scrawled on
the back of the photo frame.

My dearest darling Tom.
Happy first Christmas.
Lots of love mummy and daddy. XXX

The picture mysteriously evolved. The parents disappeared from view as if they were never there. The boy grew up. The small window gushed open with an unpredictable burst of wind. The picture was back hanging up on the wall. Tom was nowhere to be seen. Unless you gazed closely at the photo. He was the boy.

Trapped forever.

The Clock
by Emma Asiedu

After school, Mike was walking home and something caught his eye. Mike was looking at an abandoned mansion. The mansion was huge but very broken. The windows were smashed, the door was broken, and the decaying roof was breaking in front of his eyes. Mike didn't know what to do, whether he should explore the mansion or just ignore it and go home but curiosity got the better of him. Mike got closer and closer to the mansion; he opened the door.

Mike looked around the mansion. Half of the house was broken-he looked further. The house was damaged. It looked like the people who lived there didn't take care of the place. As Mike walked through the house, he stumbled across a kitchen, a big kitchen. The kitchen was full of dust and rust and there was a half-eaten dinner on the table; it was disgusting.

As Mike walked thought the kitchen, there was a loud noise. Mike walked into the living room. The living room was huge. There was a 32 inch TV, there was a big plant and a table. The sofa was big enough to fit 10 adults. As Mike was exploring the living room there was another loud noise but this time it was upstairs. So Mike went upstairs.

As Mike walked up stairs, there was a creek. To his left was the bedroom. Mike decided to go to the bathroom first. Mike tiptoed to the bathroom. This bathroom was big but it was also broken. The bathtub was broken, the toilet was broken and the drain was broken.

After Mike finished inspecting the bathroom, he went straight into the bedroom. Mike walked into the bedroom; it was astronomical. Mike said to himself, "This room is huge." The bed was big and comfy with big puffy pillows and the wardrobe was as big as an elephant. Then there was another noise but this time this one was in the attic. The Attic was too high for Mike to get up. Mike didn't know what to do but in the corner of his eye there was a wooden broomstick. So Mike used the wooden broomstick to get the trap door open. Mike's heart skipped a beat as he climbed up the ladder. Mike was amazed; there was so much stuff. There were clothes, chairs, tables, paint and books. But the only thing that caught Mike's eye was this clock. The clock was very dusty, narrow and decaying. It looked like this clock had been through a lot in this house. Mike got closer and closer to the clock. He touched the clock and saw glimpses and memories of people he loved. Ticking, ticking, ticking...

Mike was trapped inside the clock.

For Now Game Over
by Frankie Johnson

'Game Over' - Sam hated that phrase but he was overjoyed because he was playing his favourite game: PAC-MAN. As Sam and Zack walked home, they started talking about the thing they loved most: video games.

"Pac-man is definitely the best game because it is so exciting and challenging because you can never win but you can always improve!" exclaimed Sam.

"No! Centipede is definitely the best and you know it!"Zack answered.

"I got to go now but can you come to mine tomorrow?" questioned Sam.

As Sam walked in his house, his mom was waiting for him.

"Where have you been young man!" snapped his mum.

"At the arcade," stammered Sam.

"Go to your room!" shouted his mum.

"It's half eight!" raged his mum.

Sam ran upstairs and left a trail of muddy footprints to the room. Sam didn't care about getting told off; so he got out his favourite present: a Pac-man handbook which had all the tips and tricks to being the world's best Pac-man player. When Sam woke up, in the morning, he stared at the alarm clock for what seemed like an hour. He must have been up all night because it was an hour past the opening of his school so he sprang out of his bed like a kangaroo and ran to his wardrobe. He put on his uniform, ran down to the kitchen and on the table was a letter, from his mum and two rounds of toast. The letter read:

Hopefully you have a great day and concentrate on work and not Pac-man. Love you lots Mum.

Sam ran out of the door not even noticing Zack wasn't there. As Sam ran past the arcade, he saw a person waiting at the doors of the arcade. The person had denim jeans and a coat that had a grey pixelised logo on the back. Sam noticed it was a pixelised centipede. One thing Sam was intrigued about was he had his hood up and it wasn't even raining. Oblivious Sam walked on and trudged to school. When he got to school, he ran into class. He looked around for Zack but he wasn't at his seat.

His teacher glared at him and pointed at his desk. As Sam glared longingly at the clock, he had an idea. He would pretend to be sick so he could go to the arcade. He did a somersault in his head. He raised his hand in the air and then when his teacher finally acknowledged him and asked what seemed to be the problem, Sam started to explain that he felt like was going to be sick and if he could go home. The teacher stared at him for a brief moment. Then the teacher said he should go to the office and they would send him home.

After they checked he could walk home by

himself, they let him go. Suddenly it started to hail. It cascaded to the ground. Sam walked out of the main entrance and fled to his house. He couldn't believe it had worked; he scrambled up the stairs to get changed but when he got up to his room he stared at the same spot for at least a minute. His handbook had moved. He must have moved it this morning.

When he had scampered down to the front door and ran out, the weather had got worse. He ran as fast as he could, until he got to the Arcade. As he walked in to the air conditioned entrance, he smiled and pushed open the doors to the arcade. He strode over to the Pac-man machine and he started to play. After about a minute of playing, he started to feel dizzy and his head began to spin ...

He was trapped inside PAC-MAN? There was only one way to find out. He started to run but when he looked down he saw yellow pixels. All around him was blackness then a glowing light started to come nearer and nearer BOOP!!!!BOOP!!!!!BOOP!!!!!

For now GAME OVER

by Hollie Hearne

Max was a short boy. He had long hair, just above his shoulders and freckles all over his face. His most favourite clothes to wear were his denim jacket with a striped long-sleeved shirt, his skinny jeans and some red trainers. He was only 15 years old. He lived in a small town where he loved to go on walks. Max had lovely parents, Jimmy and Tina; they spoilt him a lot. He also had a best friend in school called Jamie- they had been best friends since pre-school. Max had a passion for painting. In his spare time he would paint the most wonderful pictures. Max's most favourite thing to paint was the sunset. Every night he would dream about becoming a famous artist.

It was Monday and it was like another boring day. He had to go to school, cook dinner and do his homework. As usual he had finished his homework quickly so he had time to go upstairs and work on his painting. When he was upstairs, he heard his mum and dad come home from work. "Maxie we're home!" shouted his mum. "How was your day?" asked his dad. "It was great thanks Dad!" replied Max.

Finally dinner was ready. They sat down

together at the table. "Me and your mum have been talking and we have decided that this house is getting quite old now..." said his dad. "And we have decided to move house next week," continued his mum.

"What!" Max shouted. Max went upstairs and carried on painting. He forgot what happened. KNOCK! KNOCK! KNOCK! It was his mum and dad. "Come in!" Max shouted. They opened the door and sat on his bed. "We are very sorry that we have to move," began his dad. "We also have some more bad news," said his mum. Max's mum hesitated. "You will also have to move schools too!" Max's mum continued.

Max woke up really early: he was really nervous about telling Jamie. How was he going to tell him? At 6:00 am, Max got up and got ready for school. When he got to school, he didn't want to tell Jamie yet. Unfortunately, he bumped into him on the way to his first class. "Hey Maxie! How are you?" asked Jamie. "I'm fine thanks. I have got to talk to you," began Max. "Ok, what is it?" asked Jamie. "Well, I am moving house next week..." continued Max. "Oh cool!" Jamie said excitedly. "Unfortunately, that means I will have to move schools," Max replied tearing up. "Good luck for next week! I have to go to class. Talk to you later," Jamie shouted walking to class. Max looked at the time and he had to go to class too. He felt really bad for Jamie. Wiping away his tears, Max walked into his class.

It was his last day at his school and Max and Jamie were still best friends. Everyone was signing Max's t-shirt and making him good luck cards. At the end of the day, Max felt very popular. At the end of the day, they both hugged, said their last goodbye and went home. They missed each other already.

It was the next day. Max was going through his toys and clothes ready to give them away to charity. He was packing everything and saying his last goodbyes to his house. The moving van had arrived to pick up everything so he helped his parents. When they had done, they set off on their car journey.

Max's face dropped. It was a horror story. He couldn't believe his eyes. "Is this our house?" Max asked his parents crossing his fingers. "Yes Maxie," his mum replied. "Oh no," Max whispered to himself. "Do you like it?" asked his dad. He just ignored him because he didn't want to offend his parents. Max opened the car door and jumped out. The clouds turned black and it looked like it was going to rain. BANG! Rain began to pour down. Thunder began to crash. The whole family ran inside their new house.

Inside was cold. It looked like it hadn't been cleaned in decades. The front door was red and scratched and the carpet needed to be hoovered. As you walked in, you could see an old wooden stair case in front of you. There was a small, crumby table under the stairs along with a giant door that lead under the stairs. Beside the stairs was a long arch way leading to the living room. It had three long couches. The TV was old fashioned and the paintings were ancient. Through the other arch way was the kitchen. The kitchen floor had holes in it. The counters were scratched and crumby. In the kitchen there was a round, dusty table with four wooden chairs around it. Max hated his new house already. He had only seen the downstairs.

Max decided to explore upstairs. It wasn't

much different. His mum showed him his room; it was humungous. There was a door in his room that he tried to open but it was locked. He searched for a key but there was no sign. BANG! Woosh! Creak! The wind had opened the large window in his room. It had made him jump. Max went to shut the window and looked outside. There was a huge storm.

Max put on his uniform and looked in the mirror. He looked so smart. His tie was striped blue and black and his jumper was black with his school logo. His mum dropped him off at the school gates and he nervously walked in. As he walked into reception, everyone was staring and pointing at him. There was a boy that said hi to him on his way in. He looked at his schedule and he had science first. Max walked in and sat at a desk with no one on it. Then, the boy he had passed in the corridor came and sat down at his desk.

"Hi. What is your name?" asked the boy. "My name is Max," replied Max shyly. "My name is Leo. Nice to meet you," said Leo. "Why don't you come over to my house after school," suggested Max. "Ok!" replied Leo excitedly. "There is a door in my room that is locked, why don't we try and open it!" said Max

After school, Max and Leo walked home together. When they got home, Max shouted up to his mum who was working in the office. "Mum, I'm home!" shouted Max.

"Hi, how was school?" asked his mum. "I made a new friend. Is it alright if he stays for tea?" asked Max. "Yes of course," his mum shouted back. They rushed upstairs and Max gave Leo a house tour. Max showed Leo his room and it was massive. They just chatted for a bit and got to know each other. Whilst they were chatting, the door in Max's room flung open and made them jump. BANG! "AHHH!" they both screamed.

Max and Leo slowly and gently walked towards the door and peeked in. They both looked at each other with a confused look on their faces. "You go down first," Leo said. "No you, I'm too scared," replied Max. "It's your house," Leo shouted. There was a silent pause. "Fine, I will go first!" Max gave in and huffed. Max led the way down the creepy staircase. Then Leo followed slowly behind him. They carried on down the stone staircase: it lead to a mysterious room of paintings. Max walked over to all of the paintings in disbelief. He wished he could paint just like these paintings. There were many different things on the paintings such as flowers, people and animals. There was one painting that caught Max's attention. It had a dirty cloth over it. Max took off the cloth and his jaw dropped. It was so detailed. He took one step towards the painting and started to feel dizzy.

"I think we should go now," Max said worriedly. "Ok, it's really scary in here anyway," replied Leo. Max turned around but he couldn't move. "I can't move! Help!" shouted Max. Leo ran to help but when he went to help he couldn't move either. "I'm stuck too!" Leo shouted. "AHH!" they both screamed. The painting had opened up and they were getting sucked in. "Dinners ready!" Max's mum shouted. No reply. "Are you boys ok?" asked his mum.

Still no reply. She came upstairs and knocked on Max's door. They didn't reply. She went in and saw no one in there but the mysterious door open.

"Oh no!" shouted Max's mum.

Trapped
by Isaac Davies

The plane took off.

"Why do we have to move," said James.

"Because your dad has a new job," said Mary - James's mum.

"But I had lots of friends in England," said James.

James was eleven years old and very tall and skinny. He had blue eyes and loves reading. James was very adventurous and loves going on adventures. When they arrived, they found it an old ramshackle house wedged in-between two tall skyscrapers.

They opened the front door and saw loads of cobwebs. There was an old, creepy staircase with a rotting banister.

Mary said, "We need to clean this up."

"But can't we sleep. We have been travelling for ages," said James.

"The quicker we work the sooner we can sleep," said Mary.

They both got out the

cleaning brushes and started cleaning. James had a lot of work to do - it was making him even more tired. Eventually his mum let him sleep. When he woke up he realised that his mum had cleaned the whole house.

James was looking round the house when he saw a ladder to the attic. James pulled down the ladder and climbed up.

The attic was a big room with windows in the roof. Cobwebs covered the walls; boxes were stacked along the wall. James opened a box. He saw that there were lots of toy soldiers. He was about to pick one up, when his mum called him down for food.

James rushed to the table and scoffed down his food. He then ran upstairs to the attic.When James got to the attic, it started to rain.

BOOM!

The soldiers were still there. James reached in and went to grab one.

BOOM!

The thunder made James jump. He walked back to the soldiers and picked one up.

BOOM!

The storm was getting worse, but that was not thunder. James looked around; everything had grown. James tried to step forward. He couldn't move. He looked down. He was a toy SOILDER...

Feather

by Isaac Stevens

Bang! Bang! Bang! This was the third time this week Leta's parents had locked her in the basement. Leta loved her Mum and Dad but she was too disruptive and they loved work more than her. And on top of that they moved house last month and she was finding it hard to make friends. Bang! Bang! Bang! She had only been in there five minutes but it felt like hours. When they finally let her out she went straight to bed.

"Goodbye," Leta said to herself. Her parents left for work at four in the morning so she woke herself up for school. She hated her school uniform. It was her least favourite colour ... pink. She didn't even know you could get pink school uniform. The logo was nice though. It was a swan feather. Leta closed the door behind her and walked down an alleyway. The alley was surprisingly long but half way down she noticed a shop. It was a shop like no other. It looked cold; it was ominous. The window was covered by a wooden plank and a big feather on the roof.

Leta's curiosity took over. She walked in. A bell rang, "Ding!" She looked around and was about to leave when she heard something. Walking into an empty room, she noticed a shelf but all the books had been pushed onto the dilapidated wooden floor. Leta was cold; she was afraid. Looking around one last time, she noticed a dream catcher but this one looked beautiful. It was an ebony black with white feathers hanging from the base. Leta ran to the shelf, grabbed the dream catcher and just caught the bus for school.

Leta traipsed to the bus stop with reluctance in her heart. The journey was a nightmare. It started to rain so she was soaking by the time she got to the bus. But when she got home her parent's car wasn't there. After three minutes of searching for her key, she used the back door and went up to her room. She hung up her dream catcher and got into bed.

Leta woke up sweating. She had the most strange dream. She was stuck in the dream catcher. Looking around, she noticed it still hanging on the shelf. She had goose bumps all over. Leta walked over to the dream catcher, reached her arm out and "whoosh" she was shot up into the air then gently floated down and spun round like a tornado then finally she was sucked into the dream catcher. Now where was she ... TRAPPED!!!

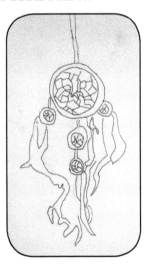

Trapped

by Isla Hillis

There were two girls. They were sisters, twins, best friends and they did everything together. Sofia had long brown hair and Ruby had short blond hair and they both had crystal blue eyes.

The girls had a big interest in books and always went to the library. And one day they decided to go. It was old; the door wasn't working properly because the hinge was coming off. It was dusty and full of cobwebs. The shelves were stacked high with books. The chairs had no legs and they were sitting on the floor, but they still went in.

When the girls got into the library, they tried to find a book to read. Then an old lady came up to them and handed them a book. They went and sat in the corner (in this case the worst place to sit) and at the same time they read out the name together. It said trapped. Then a random lady came up to them and shouted at them. She said that they were not allowed to read the book and they said that a lady gave them the book to read but the lady did not believe them so they gave her the book and ran out of the library.

The next day, the girls came back to the library. They wanted to read and know more about the book. Sofia snuck the book under her jacket.

"What are you doing? You can't steal," Ruby whispered.

"I'm not stealing it. We're going to read it in the corner," said Sofia

"Then why are you hiding it?" said Ruby.

"You don't want to get shouted at by that lunatic again do you?" said Sofia sarcastically.

"True, fine then, come on let's go," said Ruby.

The girls went into the corner. It was dusty but they didn't care. They started reading it. But amazingly the book started to glow. Before they knew it the book was floating up; they started screaming and the book fell down. The girls had disappeared... and were never seen again. As for the lady, she was sacked for shouting at innocent little girls and the girls remained lost forever.

The House
By Javannah Jatta

Slam went the door as I stormed in the kitchen. "Guess what Mum? I just got fired for nothing I did!" I moaned. "Well it's not my fault. You did it!" argued Mum. I stood up and stormed to the stairs then my dad came in. "Oh here we go again," I mumbled. As my dad walks in, he tells me to go to my room so I did.

When I got to my room, I heard crying and screaming next door. I went to look in the window and there was an old man who I had never seen before. I yelled are you ok? Then he just stopped and stared at me. I called my mum but she said nobody was in so I pulled her to the window but she said, "I can't see anyone so you are hallucinating." So I went to bed but I didn't sleep most of the night. The next morning, I woke up coughing my guts out. I walked down stairs. My mum said, Stay home. Have some porridge. I will go shopping."

But the one specific word she said was to leave next door alone but I didn't want to. I wanted to go over so I got my shoes on and walked to the front of my house. I looked through the window to see if anyone was in the house. I went behind the house to the garden. The door was locked so I rang the door bell and waited two minutes, 30 minutes and there was still no sign of the old man so I kicked down the door. It was hard but the house looked gross. There was a puff of dust going straight in my face. It was not nice. I swore nobody lived in the house. There was no light in the house so I walked upstairs to see what else there was and... I walked back down. I couldn't. I was too scared and walked back home.

I got very suspicious on the way back. I heard footsteps echoing behind me and so I ran into the bush with the thorns scraping my skin. The man showed up in front of the bush. I got my phone out and started videoing but my flash was on. He saw me but I was too scared. I blacked out. I woke up to a loud smash of glass. I finally got a blur of where I was. There was a shiver down my spine. All I could see was the old man staring right at me. I was traumatised. My heart skipped one billion beats. He opened his wrinkly mouth and said, "You can't run, you are trapped like your brother." He told me I could never escape because if you do you will end up like your brother. I was too scared. I passed out.

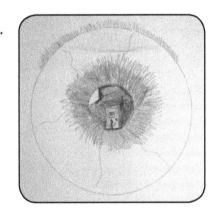

I could see what he was on about. But he never knew my brother. He went missing before the man moved in. Now my brother has been missing for years. Oh I miss him. But I can't go. I'm out of time. I'm stuck in a glass room with the shiniest window ever. I give up. There's no point of trying.

By Lara Buckingham

Small town, England, 1944

As the Spitfires arrived, the town held its last breath. A curious, young boy-whose name was Oliver-took shelter behind a black umbrella. He peeked from behind it praying the Spitfires had left. His head turned to an abandoned library, surely a perfect place to hide for now. Oliver slowly twisted the rusted handle and the door creaked open in reply. Musty air spilled out like a broken tap; never ending. Oliver crept across the wooden floor; stroking the spines of books as he went. The door slowly locked behind him.

He went into a panic. Mind racing, he slammed his fists against the door: begging to be heard. But the streets were empty. Fog surrounded the window panes like guards forcing him back. The dust choked him at the back of his throat. "I must get out," he said gasping for breath. "Help me." He opened his mouth meaning to shout for help but nothing came out. It was as if it tugged him by the back of his throat; pulling him deeper in its iron grasp. Oliver sat against the barricaded window-the rough wood scraping his skin. He clutched his side as a tear rolled down his cheek. Would he ever see his family again?

As Oliver attempted to stand up, the clocks arms struck twelve and the doors bell began to chime. He stood there as cold as ice, his heart quickened until... The world seemed to spin away. Strange noises filled his head. He heard voices, voices gasping for help. Oliver could hear the cries as the glass smashed on the marble tiles and the water as it dripped from the stalactites. It was as if the water drained away all hope or joy that ever filled this place. Maybe it was just a nightmare? Maybe he would wake up in bed to the chirping of crows. Doubts crowded his mind like a swarm of bees.

Oliver's eyes slowly opened, he was back in the library, back on the cold floor. A bright light flashed across the wood, daring him to come closer. He searched the hundreds of books that cluttered this place. But he could not locate the source.

"Where is it?" Oliver thought. "There has to be a way out, maybe I should follow the light?" He ducked under a large cabinet. The light poured out from behind the skirting. Oliver dug his finger nails in the side of the board. And just like that it rolled aside. He crept in unsure of what he had just discovered. An old chandelier loomed over the boxes and papers that surrounded him. They were all cloaked in white sheets that looked like ghosts at every corner.

His eyes turned to an old wooden chest with a rusted lock that clanked as he stepped on a floor board. The light flickered off the chest as he pushed open the lid. The sight he saw was hypnotizing. He looked into the chest and dug around for a clue or something about who owned this place. He lifted up a gold hourglass; it flickered and shined in the misted mirrors. Red sand filled the bottom. It lay on the cool glass like freshly fallen snow. In the bottom was the initials O.C. He slowly pressed his fingers against the engraving. He felt his soul leave him pulling him down.

He felt as if he was falling, falling into an abyss. Red flashed across his eyes as he fell. Down, down. Oliver felt for the creaky floorboards but they weren't there. It had been replaced with sand, red sand. He slowly stood up; he was surrounded by glass. His eyes adjusted to the dark and what he saw made his blood run cold. Millions of people: trapped in hourglasses; trapped in time. But what was done was done. Who had done this? A stained glass window of a man grew a wicked smile. A cackle so hard and cruel shattered the glass like an avalanche.

Oliver's time had run out and you're next...

Lost for Life

by Laura Armstrong

The bell rang. Sophie and Matilda grabbed their coats and ran out of the school while eating donuts. So they ran off to the grand library in the centre of the town, where people would gather together to celebrate Christmas, Halloween, the Queen's birthday, and Easter. Sophie and Matilda always wear the same t-shirts every day. They even look like twins except from their hair. Sophie would have long, curly ginger hair. Matilda would have brown hair like some people in her classroom even though they were sisters.

Sophie and Matilda walked around the water fountain and found pennies that would sparkle in the sun-light every day. Their favourite place is Sprinkle Ice Cream because the ice cream there is one of the best and the ice cream would be covered with sprinkles of every colour. The library was magnificent. The walls were covered with the world's most famous authors: J.K. Rowling, Roald Dahl, David Walliams and Peter Bunzl. But there was something strange about the library. In one aisle the lights were flickering and the window slammed right down making the book shelf wobble. Even one of the books fell off. Lost. The book was called LOST FOR LIFE. Sophie went to pick it up.

The book gave Sophie a shock. She fell right onto her back. She felt like she was fading away into the wooden planks. "Sophie, Sophie, wake up," said Matilda. The bookkeeper [Oliver] heard a thud.

THUD!

"Hello, hello," said Oliver.

Sophie stood up and explained what happened. But the bookkeeper seemed okay with it strangely enough. Oliver just realised what book it was. He said, "Oh sorry but you can't take this book home... at all!"

"Why?" said Matilda.

"Because," whispered Oliver. Sophie and Matilda walked out not liking the library any more. A few hours later, Sophie and Matilda waited for everyone to go to sleep and the library to close down. After they got up and changed into black clothes, they tip-toed down the stairs and got a quick snack then snuck out to the library. All of the shops were closed. The whole road was pitch–black; it was like the whole town was empty. But there was a lamppost that flickered on and off.

"There's the library," whispered Matilda, while they were looking at the lamppost. "Come on."

"Are you sure about this?" said Sophie.

"Yes...of course I am. I've broken into

your house before. You didn't notice," whispered Matilda.

"What?"

"Come on."

"All right then but if we go to jail, I am blaming it on you," said Sophie.

"We need a rope, a hammer, a ladder, and a smoke bomb."

"Why? We can just open the door."

"Fine."

So they opened the door and switched the light on. They searched the whole of the library. But Lost for Life wasn't there. But they didn't check the secret room where Oliver kept all his secret stuff. They checked all the drawers except for one.

"Let's hope the key is in here," whispered Matilda.

"Okay."

"Yes!"

"Shuuuuuuuuuuuuuuuuush," said Sophie.

"Okay."

"Open the chest, get the book and run."

Before Matilda grabbed it, she replaced the book with the orange.

"What are you doing?" said Sophie.

"I'm changing it with an orange."

"Why?"

"Because," said Matilda. A few seconds later, an alarm rang off.

"RUN!"

Oliver the bookkeeper lives right next to the library. So Oliver woke up, put his slippers on and ran as fast as he could. But before he got to the library they were gone...

Oliver looked around the whole library but there was no sign of them anywhere except for the key. Oliver found his gold key right in the centre of the library. Sophie and Matilda ran home. They were panting with fear.

"That was close," said Matilda.
They got home, ran upstairs to the attic. They sat on the carpet like they were meditating and opened the book slowly. A glimpse of sunlight shone bright in their eyes. Sophie and Matilda kept flicking through the book until they got to the end. There was an eye staring right at them.

"Let's just go Matilda."
"No, the eye just blinked."
"What do you mean?" said Sophie.
Sophie walked down the stairs and said, come on."
But there was no answer, "Come on."
Still no answer ....
Sophie walked up the stairs.

"Matilda where are you?"
The eye blinked. Sophie looked everywhere but there was no sign. The eye blinked again. Sophie saw a glance of Matilda's face.

"Matilda," said Sophie.
Matilda was trapped. Sophie was wondering what to do. She only had one idea to go to sleep and walk to library tomorrow. The next day Sophie walked to the library.

"Oliver, Oliver, where are you?" said Sophie.
Oliver appeared out of thin air. Sophie told Oliver. He was so frustrated.

"You took the book," said Oliver.
"We had to."
"Just come with me."
"Ok."
Oliver opened the book slowly.
"DON'T," said Sophie.

The eye blinked...

Oliver was gone in thin air. Sophie was freaking out. Sophie ran home and asked her mum what to do. But she didn't believe it. She was frustrated. She had no clue. Sophie ran up and down her stairs. Bing. Sophie had an idea. She went to the attic. She sat down. She opened to the middle of the book and a folded piece of paper flung out. She opened it. For some reason there were instructions about the eye at the end of the book.

1. Sit in private room.
2. Sit in the centre of the room on a carpet.
3. Sit alone.
4. And cross your legs and say eye, bring this world back to life. Eye bring these people back to life.

She said it. The clock struck at midnight. Sophie was upset. She walked down the attic stairs. BING. "Matilda, Matilda, is that you?" said Sophie. She walked up the stairs with excitement. They hugged with joy.
"Thanks for noticing me," said Oliver.
"Oh, sorry."
Everyone went back to their houses and got a good night sleep.

The Tree House from Nowhere

by Lilly Barrett

In the morning, Rose got out of her soft comfy bed. She got changed for the day and there she heard a knock on the door: it was her friend for her birthday party. So Rose and her friends got in the car then mum drove to the beach. So off they went; it was an hour away. After the hour journey, they got out of the car and ran to the beach. Above them were white greedy seagulls flying around. Rose's swimming costume had polka dots on it. Bethan her BFF-who is funny- has stripes on her swimming costume. Olivia her other BFF-who makes Rose laugh-has a flower on her swimming costume. Lilly her bestie had a pink costume.

They went to have lunch. Rose had a cheese sandwich and salad. Olivia and Bethan had a ham and cheese sandwich, Lilly had salad then her mum had a chicken wrap. After, they went to get donuts with sugar and Nutella.

"These donuts are amazing," said Lilly
So off they went down the hot burning path, down the old tattered steps. Rose, Bethan, Olivia and Lilly ran down then all went to do different things. Olivia and Lilly went and made each other mermaids with the sand and then went in the sea. Rose and Bethan got their snorkels on and went into the cool sea.

Down in the sea, not far down, Rose and Bethan went to find fish and take pictures.

"It was amazing down there!" shouted Bethan.

"Mum we found lots of fish!" said Rose. Whilst they were still talking, the sea suddenly changed turquoise.

"Kitty there is a tree house over there. Can we go and see it?" asked Olivia.

"That wasn't there earlier when we came but yes we can and you have to follow my rules," told Kitty.

"Ok," the children whispered. So off they went to down the tree house.

There was a tiny doorway and a key on the grass and then suddenly they got the key and opened the door CREEK. They slowly climbed the noisy stairs.

"Stay away from everything that might be dangerous," whispered Kitty. They went through corridors and found a room and saw an old, tattered, cracked window and found on the floor next to the bed a shell necklace. Rose showed her mum and she put it on her neck then suddenly felt a pull into the necklace then the necklace fell to the floor ...

Trapped Inside
by Lili Perring

One summer morning, Adam, an ordinary
eleven year old boy, was left home alone. He was
the only child and never got to meet his dad. He was
confused. Where was his dad? What did he look like?
Adam's mom never mentioned him and weirdly
there were no pictures of him around the house. The
house was big and old fashioned. He wasn't allowed
on a certain part of the house. It was hard for him
because he liked to explore and be adventurous but
he listened to his mom.

One nippy afternoon his mom said:

"I'm going to meet my friends at the new
lunch place in town ok?"

"Ok, Mom. How long will you be?" asked
Adam.

"I will be about an hour or two. I'm going
shopping."

"Ok, bye have fun," Adam said softly.

"Bye sweetie, be good."

Off she went–the car engine roared. Half an
hour later and he got bored. The Wi-Fi went out and
he had nothing to do. He had an idea what was on
the other side of the house. What is she hiding? He
wanted to explore. He turned on the top of his heels
and followed his nose.

He started exploring; cobwebs filled the halls and dust bundled together on the shelves. A tingle down the boy's spine gave him a fright. He was confused. What was going on he thought to himself? Nervous, he ran desperately. The door stood tall in front of him. Adam was anxious. The door swung open: SCREECH. As he jumped back he stared in. It was dark and gloomy. Flick, the light came on. Curious, he stepped in. Looking round, he was puzzled. The hall was long, and tiring. There were no photos or paintings down this hall. Adam turned back quick-Ding Dong. It was his mom.

"ARRRRRR," the boy screamed. Running back for his life, the door slammed shut. He lay down like he had been asleep. His mom walked in.

"Hello sweetie," whispered his mom as she realised he was asleep.

"Hi mom, how was lunch and shopping?"

"It was good thank you."

It was about 10:30pm now and Adam was getting sleepy. "Adam it's time for bed," she said.

He grunted and said, "Ok Mom."

Twenty minutes later and he heard his mom go to bed. He couldn't sleep: all he kept thinking about was the hall and why he wasn't allowed there. Adam was confused and got out of bed in a flash. He shoved his dressing gown and slippers on. He ambled to the torch and then over to the old oak door. Carefully he opened the door and stepped quietly down the hall. He ran as he heard a floor-board squeak. He stopped and hesitated as he got to the door; it launched open. He went fully in this time. He got to the end. He was confused. Why is there a dead end? It was dark. He couldn't see anything. Pressing his hands onto the wall he felt a chain. In curiosity he pulled it. FLASH, stairs flew in front of his eyes. Peering up and trembling, a thought popped into his head. Why don't I come back another day? No I'm going to go up there!

Prudently, he stepped onto the shiny metal stairs. He lunged cautiously up. Suddenly he got to the top and entered the black filled room. He turned on the flash light and began to look around. There were frames and photos of his dad he thought. The only thing he knew about him was his name: it was James. He walked on and found a photo. But who was it? Adam turned and dawdled. Out of nowhere, he saw a flash of gold. Out of the corner of his eye, was a dust filled, stained old sheet. Ardently, he was over there reaching for the sheet. Further and further he could reach then gradually: SNATCH. He got it. Moving the sheet away, he saw him. He believed it was really him!

CRASH! BANG! Thunder struck. The sky was coated with grey and the air went cold. Wind gushed past as the boy stared at the painting. A scream came from the attic, HELP! The painting moved. He was alive. What was going on? He moved closer. It was him; his dad. Moving closer he tried to speak.

Screaming stay away, the boy couldn't hear him. Stay away. Stay away. The man tried his hardest but it didn't work. Adam got closer and closer. Gradually he got to the frame and halted; he stared, his eyes glistened and his mouth widened. SNATCH! The frame got him. It's got him like it got his dad. Screaming for help nothing had worked. No one could hear them and no one could get them. They were together like Adam wanted but not like this.

Giza

by Luke Sutcliffe

A long time ago, 4000 years ago actually, in the barren desert of Ancient Egypt, there was a small girl called Scorpius [better known as Shadow]. Shadow was a tomb robber. She sadly lost her parents at the hands of the pharaoh Cleopatra. She chose to be a tomb robber to steal back what the pharaohs had stolen from her. This is the story of how Shadow robbed the Pyramids of Giza...

They were colossal master pieces. They were built for the pharaohs of Ancient Egypt-and I was going to rob them. I was going to rob the Pyramids of Giza! I made my way through the deserted pyramid. I walked around bends and through

doors until I stepped on a small, grey tile: it was a trap. About five small green cobra slithered out of a little trap door in the wall and I readied my bow and shot at a little brownish one and hit it right in the heart- by the way, I'm a good archer. Two more shot at me and I grabbed my sword and cut them into pieces. The other two retreated into the darkness of the pyramid; it wasn't over yet.

I kept going through the maze and accidently stepped on a few more tiles that triggered traps like arrows and flaming walls. After a long time, 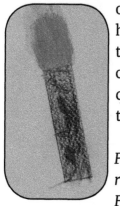 out of the corner of my eye I saw some hieroglyphics engraved on a wall. I wasn't the best with hieroglyphics although I could make out a few things. They were quite old and dusty but I could just make them out.

Find the tile with the smile and you will be rich, Touch it, tap it, and see what it does, Follow the eyes and you will be rich.

I found the tile with the smile and tapped it. Its eyes shone and rotated to look at a door. I ran over to the door and, with all my might, opened it. There in the middle of a room was a mountain of beautiful gold.I grabbed my bags and filled them with beautiful gold. I saw a small, golden goblet.

THUD, THUD, THUD! I heard footsteps and ran to the far side of the room. Left, right, right again and I finally left the pyramid- although the panic wasn't over yet. In the distance I could see a small cave. I grabbed the gold and saw a small chariot on the way so ran over to it, put the gold in and kept going."Ffuf!" I whistled for my horse and tied her to the chariot and we made it to the cave. "HEY, YOU," shouted a big guard in sandals, "GET BACK HERE."

I raised my dagger and ran at the guard. Ths, clack, bang! Out of the dark, another guard appeared. I stabbed the first, bounced back and shot the other with an arrow. I retreated back into the cave and saw the same, little goblet. I reached for my water but I didn't have any left. I went to the guard thinking at least one of them would have some and, luckily for me, they did. I poured the water into the goblet and put my lips to the rim of the cup; I drank.

AHHHHHHHH!

My face went numb and I couldn't feel my legs, body or arms. I was in the cup...`

The second city of Rome

by Olivia Tinkler

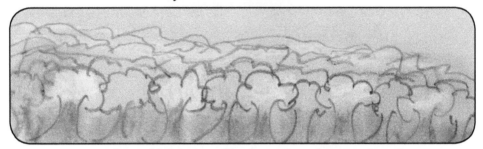

The rabbit turned a sharp bend. It sprinted through the grass; the dark trees a wide blur. His life depended on it. But his legs overtook him. He toppled over. The rabbit lay flat. His arms spread out, hoping he wouldn't get spotted.

'Father, I think we lost it,' Kelly said. 'Chief won't be happy.' She adjusted her dress and high- but short- pony tail. Kelly thought to herself: 'I'll never be a real Gaul. My legs are too short to catch rabbits.' Still looking at her Father, she went in the opposite direction towards the clearing. She misjudged her footing and tripped over the rabbit, into the bush.

'Father,' Kelly wailed. She found a hole in the bush and popped her head through. A sandal. Only Romans wore sandals. Kelly slunk back - being seven - she nosily listened in.

'Julius Ceaser said it was here,' said the one with sandals.

'Mark it on the map then.'

'You're not the General you do it.'

'Oi, it's not my fault Ceaser wants me to mark the battle co-ordinates.'

'We could beat the Gauls,'- he winced- 'without any plans.'

'Kelly, where are you?' she heard her Father shout.

'Sssh,' Kelly whispered,' listen.'

Hours later, Kelly ran round the hut. She couldn't find her Father. She was as scared as a chicken. What if the Romans had kidnapped him? Maybe he had gone to see the plans? Kelly thought if her Father had tried- surely she could try too?

Kelly entered the forbidden part of the forest. Her feet stepped on the dainty leaves; they fell from the stalk from the tiniest of a poke. She grimaced at the sight of the swamps. She made her way through the clustered mess of the arching trees. Kelly stepped on fungi- white, sticky powder exploded on to her rubber, yellow boots. Through the sudden tornado of dust, she spotted a clearing. It was filled with light. It wasn't very light at all but it was compared to the darkness of the forest. But there was a man around a campfire there. A Roman. She turned to run but it was too late: 'Come here little girl. I'm Fegonix. Don't be scared.' Fegonix's eyes glinted at the buttons on her dress.

'Actually, I'm not scared at all,' Kelly lied relieved it was a Gaul. She shuffled over to the strange man.

'Boar?' asked Fegonix. 'It's still hot. Anyway, tell me your name and where you live.' Being seven, Kelly didn't find a problem in giving away details.

'I'm Kelly Berix. I live in the Gaulish village

belonging to chief Arirdcus. I'm looking for my Father- he's gone missing.' She gobbled her boar up. It was as divine as the banquet they had on the Druid's birthday celebration. It was even better than her favourite food: bird. Kelly felt tired. She started to fall into a deep sleep:

She fell down,down,down into a tornado. The ceiling was a million miles above her. She bumped down into Rome. 'Father,' she yelled.

Kelly woke with a start. The kind man was nowhere. She rested her chin on her chest. Her buttons had gone. She had been robbed. Kelly could see the wooden wall, one hundred feet tall in the distance. She was a mouse. She ran to the gate and pushed it open. She felt her puffy dress brush against the wood. Dress. Romans didn't were dresses. They wore tunics. Kelly suddenly darted behind an ancient, parked cart. She dived- as quickly as an Olympic swimmer- inside. Into clothes. What a spot of luck! In addition, there were a lot of spare, oak planks. They could be stilts! A few minutes later, a rich landlord emerged from were Kelly had been lying. Kelly ran up to a General and asked directions for the house of tents. He dismissively waved his hand at a wall of brick.

Moonlight poured into the courtyard. It illuminated the snow white pillars. The contemporary, bright roof was made of red roof tiles. It looked like a Roman hotel. Kelly had spent some time persuading the guards, who told her she couldn't because there was an important model in there, to let her in. It would be her naptime if she were at home. But she wouldn't risk sleeping. She unbolted the state-of-art-door into a labyrinth of passages. In what felt like hours, she finally gave in. Kelly shuffled through the door saying 'PRIVATE

CLOSET'. When Kelly walked through the closet she realised it certainly was NOT a closet. Inside was a rectangular table the size of Goliath. It was weighed down with hills and shops. A model of Rome. It was dotted with crosses. She imagined the tiny people. She could reach the new found galaxy. It was hers! Everything Kelly needed. She began to trace the crosses.

BANG! She fell down down down. The ceiling was a thousand miles above her. She toppled over.

'GAUL!!!!' someone yelled.

'What?' Kelly wondered; staring up at crowds of people going about their leisure.

'Don't worry she's mine. SLAVE, COME HERE!' said a familiar voice.

'I'm not your slave,' Kelly said stubbornly as she was pulled behind a shield shop.

'You saw the model,' the voice said.

'Well done... wait, dad?' Kelly said.

'Oh, Kelly, we're in Rome,' he said.

'How? Can we go home?' she questioned.

'Yes,' was the reply. 'Once we find out how.'

Stuck

by Riland Mobey

One day, I was on my way to ancient Egypt [on a ship].The sun was out and the ocean was an alluring, turquoise colour. I saw the powerful, rough waves crashing against the rocks. After a while I started to see land.

"It's Egypt," I shouted at the top of my lungs.

Finally we're here - it was so hot. As I walked down the stairs of the boat, sweat dripped down my head. It was so hot. I already started to feel dehydrated. So I took a sip of my water and carried on. We got in the car and drove to the ancient part of Egypt. As we drove, the sand kept on getting deeper and deeper. It was hard to get through. We found the pyramids; they were huge. I headed towards them. I was so hot I didn't think I could make it. About five minutes later, we got there. I opened the huge doors and suddenly a bunch of wind blasted right through me.

A few seconds later, I went in; it was one of the darkest places I've ever seen. Luckily, I had a torch. As I walked down the pyramids hall-way, I saw a load of ancient stuff like old paintings and sarcophagi. I walked further into the pyramid when eventually I found two locked doors. So, I started looking around for a key or a code. Then I realised the hole in the wall. It could be in there. I started running towards it. I looked inside and the key was there. I was quite nervous to put my hand in, because there could be something else in there. I did it anyway. I had the key but, I didn't know what door I should go through. I went for the right because it looked more promising. Five minutes later, I found a golden sarcophagus. It was very shiny: very, very shiny. I couldn't believe what I was seeing. There was a note on top of it that said: Do Not touch my coffin otherwise you will witness a terrible curse. I called John and told him all about it. He said he'd be right there. As quick as a flash, he came zooming towards me.

I shouted, "Stop!"

But he couldn't. Two seconds later, he crashed into me and we both fell on to the sarcophagus. But nothing happened. We started

running back to the entrance. Then suddenly, something started pulling me and my friend in, sucking us through the sky. Then all I could see was black.

The House

by Rory Greenstreet

Jack and Sonny were walking along and a mist descended on the woods. Every single step they took the leaves crunched under their feet. Then, unexpectedly, Sonny stumbled over a log. Jack went to see if he could get help but he was in the middle of gloomy, abandoned woods so no-one was around.

As he wandered a bit more, he noticed an unearthly ramshackle house. A spine-chilling wind ran down his neck. He felt like he was being watched. He nervously approached the door and knocked. No answer. He knocked again. Still no answer. He tried to open it and found it wasn't locked. The door creaked open and he ventured in.

He stopped and peered around. There were cobwebs everywhere and spiders crawling across the dusty floor. He saw a sinister looking doll staring at him; he ignored it and walked away. Jack climbed the slowly rotting staircase and realised there were about ten rooms upstairs. He tried the first door. Locked. The second door swung open easily.

There was an empty bed with the covers pulled off in there. There was a flickering lamp in the corner of the room. Then he saw muddy footprints that led to the window and so he went to the garden to investigate but there were no footprints at all. This house was very mysterious. He trudged back to the house. He was hoping to find more footprints but he couldn't. All he could find was a crazily overgrown garden. As he walked inside again, he tripped over a carpet. And a bit of a trap door was revealed. He lifted it up and climbed down the ladder. There was a huge library at the bottom. Finding there was nothing there, he climbed back up the ladder and pushed the trap door but he couldn't open it. He was stuck.

He climbed down the ladder once more and strolled around the great big, underground library until he tripped over a loose floorboard and hit his head on a bookshelf. It fell over and uncovered a secret door. This house was getting more and more mysterious. The key had been left in the keyhole. He unlocked the door and went in.

There was another library. It was not quite as big as the other one, but still huge. There was a dim light glowing from the ceiling. All the books in there were older and dustier than the ones in the main library. They were very thick Jack noticed. Whoever owned this house must read a lot. He saw a book on an old wooden table with a picture of a park with a man walking his dog and a bench with no-one sitting on it. He touched to turn the page and something very strange happened: it seemed like he was being sucked into the book. The next thing he knew, he was on the bench next to the man and his dog. He was inside the book: TRAPPED!

Into the House

by Rose Smith

8TH OF MARCH 1952. That day was the day I met Ava Quinn. I dragged myself into the school grounds wishing I had stayed at my old school. The only reason I came to this school was to get away from that bully: Amara. The day seemed to go so slow until lunch; the lunch that changed my life for ever. I sat down −alone. I ate my sour apple that my mother packed. All of a sudden, a girl sat down; a beautiful girl. She had pale skin, baby blue eyes and golden hair.

She started babbling on about how she was on some welcoming committee.

"Slow down," I said quickly in hope she would stop talking. "What's your name?" I said.

"Ava and yours is?"

"Ella-May," I said.

She was amazing. She loved books, she was smart and beautiful. I told her that I was decorating my room as I had just moved here and she could come round to my house and help. So that was that. My new best friend that I met five minutes ago was coming to my house.

When I got home with Ava, I found Pa sitting at the dinner table reading the newspaper and mother cooking supper. My parents are the simple type, quiet but caring. A basic family: mother cooks, cleans and goes to afternoon tea with her friends that say I'm cute. But Pa has a new job as the bank manager so he away a lot. The only time he's home is celebrations, Fridays and Sundays. I introduced Ava to my parents and ran upstairs. I showed her to my room but sat in the middle of it was a house. A doll house. It was dirty, pink and old looking.

"What's with the doll house?" asked Ava.

"I have no idea. My older brother – Jonathan – is probably pulling some joke," I replied. "I'll go put it in the bin." I tossed it in the bin and made my way upstairs. We spent hours talking about the room and moving things around. We had so much fun. Later my parents called me down for super. Ava joined us. After tea we went upstairs. Suddenly a storm broke out and a window flew open. I rushed over and quickly closed it. Concerned, I excused myself to the bathroom.

Ella–May excused herself to the bathroom. I sat on her bed and waited. It was quiet in their house but then I heard a noise like a click or a button being pressed. I noticed the doll house was back ... and open. I had a closer look and took a couple of steps forward.

I felt a strange wind. I reached out and touched it...AHHHHHHHHHHHH. I opened my eyes but everything was different. The walls were pink, the bed was pink, and in fact everything was pink. I WAS IN THE DOLL HOUSE.

CLEO AND THE COFFIN!

by Samuel Sutcliffe

One day, a girl called Cleo, was walking out in the desert after having an argument with her parents. She was in the shade of three huge pyramids. They towered over her like a blade of grass towering over a small ant. She climbed up a tree and saw a door with hieroglyphics engraved on it. She jumped down – her linen clothes dangling behind her. THUD! She landed on the ground: her sandals hitting the sandy surface of the burning floor.

After a few minutes, she had reached the door. The wind was howling. She reached for the lever. CREEEEAK! The door slowly opened. She walked in. Then a scream. AHHHH! She had fallen. When she reached the bottom of the old room, she saw a light. The room was full of candles flickering in the dark. She stood up.

"Is anyone there?" she said into the dark – there was no reply...

She felt the wall for a sliding stone or another trapdoor. There it was- an escape route. She opened it. The passage led to a room full with doors. She entered one of the rooms. The room was large: there were walls everywhere. THUD! She was trapped: the door had shut! The walls had a thick paste on them. The walls dripped. Cleo caught some- it was poison!!!

After what seemed like hours, she saw a way out. When she arrived, she was shivering with fear- what evil lurked behind this door? Anything is better than poison. She opened the door and walked in....

She looked around; there was gold and riches everywhere. The coins glinted in the dark of the tomb. She saw gods on the walls: Anubis, Osiris. Hieroglyphics were engraved on the stone. As she walked in, she saw something. An old, dusty coffin sat there. She walked over. BANG! Something slammed on the floor behind her. It was a chest of some description.
She knelt down...

Then, as she touched the ancient, battered sarcophagus, a flash of light filled her vision: memories. Then she sat there- in the mummy- lifeless!!!

Time

by Sofia Cockle

There were two girls named Ruby and Isla. They were identical twins. Both had long blond hair and deep blue eyes. They both work at Target's new Starbucks. Ruby is younger by two minutes. They are 19. They grew up in L.A then moved to San Diego.

That morning they read in the daily magazine that an old hospital had been explored and the people had never come out. In the afternoon they went on a walk through the woods. They were about half way in, when they saw an old building. The trees around it were different. They were older and darker but the girls were curious so they went inside. Inside the place was drowning in cobwebs; there were spiders everywhere. They looked in all the rooms except one: the attic.

Isla then went into the attic to see what was there. There was a small walk-way in between walls of boxes and at the end of it was a pile of clothes that seemed to be moving. "Hey Ruby, come look at this!" said Isla. Soon Ruby got there and Isla showed her the clothes. Then there was a quaking under her feet, then a sudden scream for help.

After Isla turned around, she saw the fingertips fall through the ground. "Ruby," she yelled. "No!" That was when she decided to run to the wall. Right before she hit it, she closed her eyes, felt the feeling of falling. Then she opened her eyes and saw a spinning spiral then mountains, seas, forests, grass lands, and it all led back to the attic but it had changed. It wasn't full of boxes; it was empty. In the far distance, there were footsteps. BANG, BANG then a pause. They ran out into the hallway of the hospital. It was lit up with lights and people surrounded them but then someone walked right through them.

After that they went to the surgery room. The room had a surgery table in the middle with a side table with little knives, tweezers, scissors, and a pocket watch. Ruby didn't think they could pick anything up, but she was wrong because she tried to pick the pocket watch up. She put it around her neck and kept walking around.

She called Isla over to see the watch. Ruby then grabbed the watch. It felt like they were getting further away. Then there was a bang. The pocket watch landed on the ground and there were two little girls in it.

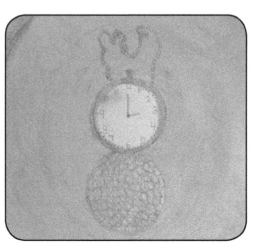

Black Hole
by Zara Mulley

2009 Oak Cottage

Hi! My name is Jennifer, aged 14. My parents are called Twiss and Dave. We are a happy family living at Oak Cottage though sometimes there are some problems. They're always going on about how dangerous attics are (they are not!) That fake things turn real (how?) and that I should never go inside one. One time I did and my parents got mad and I got grounded for 5 months. TIME FOR REVENGE!

"Jennifer. It's time for tea," Mum said last week.

"I'm coming," I would always say.

Awkwardly, I bum-shuffled down the stairs; unfortunately I slipped and banged my head on the floor. OW.

In the kitchen, there are white and black tiles on the floor, oak wood walls, grey shelves and cupboards and in the middle a shiny new table. For dinner we had my favourite: jacket potato, beans, tuna and cheese which we only have on my birthday. Overwhelmed, I sat in my seat and started lapping down my food. Once again, my parents started talking about the attic. They're always talking about it even when I ask them to stop from time to time. So I decided to go up tonight. I finished my meal, went up to my bedroom and started planning the revenge. In case you've never seen my seen my bedroom before, it's a very bright, pink room. Because I'm in love with gymnastics, I have posters, signed autographs. You're probably wondering how I've got all this: my dad's a lawyer. My bed has a purple duvet and blue cushions with stripes. I have my favourite teddy in the corner of my bed, leaning on the wall. I have shelves stacked with books: most of them are by Enid Blyton! I have a beanbag beside my bed and a T.V. opposite. I have some fish; one is called Rex and the other is Sunny. Sunny is gold and has pink dots and Rex is black with white dots.

"Jennifer have you started to get ready for bed?" my Dad said.

"Yes but not that much," I lied, but then I whispered, "Not close at all."

Dad replied, "Good I'm glad. I'll be up soon."

My dad was coming. Quick. Hide everything. I jumped into bed and pulled the duvet over me. I turned the lamp off and went to bed.

My alarm went off. I woke up; took my duvet off; put on my slippers and dressing gown, then got my torch. I started on my journey to the attic. Once I had got to the attic I looked for a box (because I couldn't reach the ladder). I looked in the kitchen, the living room, the dining room, all the bedrooms, the office, the garage, the playroom, the shed, the bathrooms, cupboards and even the utility room. Though nowhere could I find a box in the whole house! I dragged myself back to the attic. At the entrance, the ladder was still lowered because it was one of those in the ceiling. Because there were no boxes, I had to leap for it. I jumped, grabbed the ladder and pulled myself up so I started climbing the ladder.

Inside the attic, there were stacks and stacks of boxes: shoe boxes, jewellery boxes and more. No wonder there aren't any boxes in the house.

 The light started flickering then stopped working even though this house was only one year old. There were cobwebs surrounding me and so many spiders it seemed that they ruled the attic. "It's horrible up here!" I thought. "No wonder my parents hated me coming up here." There was dust everywhere so I decided to go back to my bedroom. I turned around and went for the door. IT HAD DISAPPEARED: I. Was. Trapped. I turned back with a frown on my face. But then something was there that wasn't there before...

A chest: a bright, shiny chest made out of bronze and gold, it looked like. There were patterns etched into it and crystallised, gold swirled around the corners. Stepping towards the chest there was a note on it in my B.F.F's handwriting. It had written on it, 'Open it and you will seek an amazing surprise'. Should I or should I not? Suddenly, something pushed me to the box which then opened by itself. I hoped that in it there would be what every child and every adult would dream of getting.

Though when I opened it there was a plastic, black circle with an orange ring around it and white dots just like stars. Just then, I realised what it was: a black hole that was fake. Weird I know but true.

All of a sudden, I heard my parents coming up the ladder so I dropped the toy and ran towards the boxes to go and hide in the corner of the room at the back. There was a gust of wind. I turned around. There in front of me was a real black hole in the attic. I peered down to see where the toy was but I tripped and there I was falling down.

My mum and dad came through the door due to all the noise but then back out because everything was normal. The next morning my parents had forgotten about me!

Lightning Source UK Ltd.
Milton Keynes UK
UKHW022000151019
351648UK00002BA/3/P